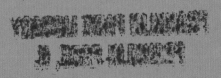

HIP & HOP, Don't Stop!

by Jef Czekaj

Disney • HYPERION BOOKS

NEW YORK

E
386-9123

Text and illustrations copyright © 2010 by Jef Czekaj

Printed in Singapore • First Edition • 1 3 5 7 9 10 8 6 4 2 • Designed by Elizabeth H. Clark • Reinforced binding • ISBN 978-1-4231-1664-6

F850-6835-09319

Library of Congress Cataloging-in-Publication Data on file. • Visit www.hyperionbooksforchildren.com

How to Read This Book!

Whenever you see this rabbit rapping
and the words are green, read as
fast fast fast as you can.

If this turtle is rapping and
you see red words, read as
s l o o o o o o o o o w l y
as you can.

This is **HOP**. You can probably figure out what kind of animal she is.

BUNNY FOR LiFE !

BREAKBEAT MEADOW

HOP'S HOUSE

SUGAR HiLLS

Hip and Hop lived in different parts of Oldskool County. But they had something in common.

They both loved to write rhymes.

Hip's raps were slower than molasses.
So slow that he made his friends sleepy.

I swim through the water.
I sleep on the rocks.
When I was three
I caught turtle pox.

I went to the doctor.
He gave me a shot.
Then I felt better,
in fact, quite a lot.

Hop's rhymes were quicker than lightning.
So quick that her friends could barely
understand her.

I take my bath
in a lake.
My favorite food
is carrot cake.

I jump to the left.
I jump to the right.
When I fall asleep,
I need a night-light.

BOOM
BOOM
CHICKA

WHAT
DID SHE
SAY?

I THINK
SOMETHING
ABOUT
A PARROT
SNAKE.

FLAP
FLAP

You might think that Hip and Hop were friends.
But they had never even met.
You see, creatures from Slowjamz Swamp
and Breakbeat Meadow didn't talk to each other.

No one could remember exactly why.
It's just the way it was.

One day, on their way home from school, Hip and Hop saw the same poster.

Then, they saw each other.

Hip and Hop didn't know what to do.

Hip was up next.

The swamp is where
I make my home.
If I had some hair
I'd use a comb.

It was getting late,

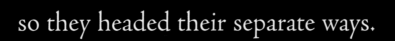

so they headed their separate ways.

The next day, Hop told her classmates about her new friend.

But Hip and Hop didn't let it bother them.
They had to get ready for the contest.

Better hurry up, because I rap quick. I'll make a beat with this dead stick.

Bang that stump in a slow groove, because I rap the way slugs move.

They practiced rhyming and listened to their favorite music.

And sometimes, they just did nothing together.

At last, the big day arrived.
It seemed like everyone from Oldskool County was there.

Two by two, they took the stage to "battle" each other with their raps.

Finally, just two contestants were left.

Hop didn't want to compete against her best friend,
but the audience was waiting. So she began.

I'm a rabbit, not a hare.
I'm a bunny, not a bear.
So get out of your chair;
wave those paws in the air.

Her rap was so fast that no
one could understand her.

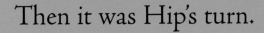
Then it was Hip's turn.

If you're a mouse,
or if you're a whale,
big or small,
just shake your tail.

He rapped so slowly
that everyone stopped
paying attention.

Things were going horribly. Luckily, Hip had an idea.

They would rap together!
First Hop took a verse,

Hip's my pal—
I'll shout it out loud.
I'm not ashamed,
in fact, I'm proud.

The crowd was stunned!
They had never heard a turtle and a rabbit rap together.

But Hip and Hop kept going.
And a funny thing happened.

First, one animal
started dancing.

Before long, another
joined in,

and then another,

and another.

Soon the whole crowd was breaking,
popping, and locking to Hip and Hop's rhymes.

When it came time to choose the winner, everyone agreed.
Hip and Hop shared the title of "Best Rappers in Oldskool County."

Hip and Hop were happy to win the contest,
but mostly they just wanted to rock the party.

And so they did . . . until way past everyone's bedtimes.